For brother Jeff, for Leah, for Neruda again,
and in memory of a horse named Lucky.   —J.L.

With love to Lorea Balzategui y la gente de Oñate, España,
and also to Victoria and Antonia.   —B.S.

Special thanks to Victoria Rock, Erica Jacobs, Susan Greenwood,
Amy Novesky, and the wonderful children's staff at Chronicle Books.

Text ©1997 by Jonathan London.
Illustrations ©1997 by Brooke Scudder.

Book design by Vandy Ritter and Suellen Ehnebuske.
Title type calligraphy by Laura Jane Coats.
Typeset in Electra.
The illustrations in this book were rendered in watercolor.
Printed in Hong Kong.

Library of Congress Cataloging-in-Publication Data
London, Jonathan, 1947-
        If I had a horse / by Jonathan London ; illustrated by Brooke Scudder.
                p.   cm.
        Summary: A child imagines riding a horse through the jungle, down the beach,
        among clouds and volcanoes, and up the sky to the moon.
        ISBN: 0-8118-1112-3
        [1. Horses–Fiction. 2. Imagination–Fiction.]   I. Scudder, Brooke, ill.
        II. Title.
        PZ7.L8432If   1997
        [E]–dc20   96-28722
                                                CIP
                                                AC

Distributed in Canada by Raincoast Books
8680 Cambie Street, Vancouver, British Columbia V6P 6M9

10 9 8 7 6 5 4 3 2 1

Chronicle Books
85 Second Street, San Francisco, California 94105

Web Site: www.chronbooks.com

If I Had a Horse

by Jonathan London ◆ illustrated by Brooke Scudder

chronicle books · san francisco

If I had a horse
I would ride through the jungle

I would pick wild fruit
and eat the sweet flesh of mangos

juice would fly and parrots scream
if I had a horse.

If I had a horse
I would gallop down the beach

I would ride a horse of sun
into the crash of the waves

flying fish would leap
if I had a horse.

If I had a horse
I would ride through the mangroves

I would ride a horse of water
through the secret maze of trees

starfish would shine
if I had a horse.

If I had a horse
I would climb the wild cliffs

I would ride a horse of rock
amid the swoop of swallows

iguanas would hide
if I had a horse.

If I had a horse
I would ride through the mountains

I would ride a horse of smoke
among clouds and volcanoes

atop the world I would be
if I had a horse.

If I had a horse
I would ride through the wind

I would ride a horse of wind
past the *publicos* and burros

wind would comb his mane
if I had a horse.

If I had a horse
I would ride a horse of rain

I would ride a horse of lightning
I would thunder down the sky

palms would bend and coconuts fly
if I had a horse.

If I had a horse
I would ride in the *carnaval*

I would ride a horse of music
through the maracas and the drums

he would dance like flames
if I had a horse.

If I had a horse
I would ride among the shadows

I would ride a horse of shadows
in a grove by the sea

the night would bloom around me
if I had a horse.

If I had a horse
I would ride in the moonlight

I would ride a horse of moonbeams
up the sky to the moon

to the moon I would ride
if I had a horse.

If I had a horse
I would ride in my dreams

I would ride a horse of dreams
and gallop through the night

his hooves would spark stars
if I had a horse.